MELANCHOLY

THE DEPRESSION

MEHREEN MANZOOR

I normally dedicate my book to depressed people's.

Contents

Melancholy

The depression

by

<u>MEHREEN MANZOOR</u>

Preface

I have thought it right to write a story which is based on depression . Because usually we get a news that someone has hanged himself or commited suicide because of family issue, social or financial problems which leads to depression and this book is also about a suicidal case. Many examples from real world events have been provided to help people connect what they have learned to their everyday lives.

i hope that you will understand and enjoy by reading this book.

Acknowledgements

Anxiety is possessing a mind that wants to die while being in a body that is fighting to survive.

This book is based on the research of youth suicidal cases. The increase in suicides in young people, mostly in poor peoples is because of social problems and unrecognised depression. Many thanks to all thode whose work, research and support helped me to write this book, especially my sibling Mehak Manzoor and my mentor Shahid Sir who had a hand in completing this book.

Most of all i want to thank my elder sister who have hand-holded me in every situation. The first draft of my book_ the one you are reading _would not have been conceivable without her, Nidah Manzoor, a courageous person who stuck by me and supported me every time.

Thank you to them and to you, reading this now..

<u>Melancholy</u>

Ever noticed how everyone in the world is cruel and self-centred? For example, the poor need money, the miserable need happiness, and parents need babies who will constantly obey them, listen to them far more than themselves, and carry out all of their wishes.

So, a similar incident happened in a house in a village. Where after many prayers, a flower emerged in a garden with high expectations from the gardener. A little girl was welcomed into the world with great joy and high aspirations, just like a tiny blossom in a garden. Her eyes were shining brilliantly like a diamond. Her saccharine smile is an inspiration for her parents with new hopes and innovativeness. Despite the fact that she has only recently been born, her parents have already set expectations on her. But because she was born after many years, many prayers and she was the only child of her parents. Her mother loves her very much, as every mother does. Her mother is more endearing when her daughter smiles, they were living a joyful life and she was treated as a princess.

"Mother's love and babies' smiles are the noblest things in this world!"

With time, she became young to play while maintaining the same purity and naivete of a newborn. Without responsibilities, worry, or anxiety, her life was flawlessly functioning without contradiction. The terms "backstabbing, jealous, and insolence" are words she isn't even familiar with. She was simply enjoying every moment of her existence as everyone does in their childhood. She was living her life as she pleased, getting up at eight in the morning to play with her friends, not caring what she lookedlike,not wearingcostly cosmetics only to cover up her natural grin, getting dirty, and returning home without fear.

She hid her arms in her blouse, pretended to have lost them, and hid behind a door while waiting to startle someone. She was oblivious to family issues, duties, stress, and melancholy. She must now attend school, interact with new people, and develop her first friendships. The day she went to school was the day she realized she was headed to a jail where the classroom was a prison and the teachers were jailers. She believed that she thought she was the saddest person in the world because of her daily commute to school, schoolwork, and other obligations. She is already lovely, but her pure mentality and innocence make her much more so. Her innocent mind makes her more beautiful than she is already but even so, she lives a wonderfully happy life with her family and friends. As she spends half of the day with her friends, she likes to be with them. Her tantrums were accepted, whatever she wants she gets it.

She is not interrupted by anyone But she will be taunted by everyone She thinks that her life is easy The wind will be extremely breezy.

"Once you've grown up, you can never come back, never."
J. M. Barrie.

The time of innocence has passed and she has just turned into an adolescent. The age when you are cognizant of everything for the first time, the time to understand how the world works, how life changes, how school works, how attracted or attracted you are to each other, etc. The teenage years are a time when self-control is required because this is the age when harmful thoughts can easily take over your head. You will be successful in the future if you have control over your life since doing the wrong thing might damage and harm your life.

She judges predicament are few Until, it comes to you
Time flies, and she grew up Her happiness slowly flew up

She is now in her teenage years and she has gotten alittlebit more mature but still, she is not mature enough to decide what is good and what is bad for her and what is right and wrong. She does things which she feels good about and which make her happy. Her parents were suffering from some financial issues and didn't have enough money to fulfil the dreams of their daughter because her father fell sick and gradually their business started sinking. Her family expects her to fix this all, she was doing her best, she used to do allthis forher family but they were not satisfied and she grew up quickly as the years passed. She used to remember her childhood memories. But at this point, she is neither a baby nor a young child. She was very much interested in studying but her family problemsmessed up allher dreams,shedidn't wantto listen to anyone but she was forced to. She aspires to work as a photographer and editor, her family does not support her since they believe that her daughter should focus on her future instead of having unrealistic expectations of becoming a photographer because such a career might lead to any profession or have any range of possibilities. She was satisfied with everything. She was just considering her future at this point, along with any issues with her family, school, or grades. She went to school one day when a nearby cobbler girl who was the same her age caught her attention as she was walking to school. They struck up a conversation and became close friends. She once questioned the girl, "Why are you polishing shoes in this day and age?" When the poor girl was asked

why she was there, she said that she is an orphan and that
her parents had left us alone.

did she say: us?

Yes, me and my sister. I am performing this sort of labor
at an age where parental responsibility is taking over
because I have a younger sister and I need to feed her and
fill her stomach; otherwise, I would want to study like
youare and sit freely in a huge house with family, without
tension and responsibilities. I don't feel any pressure since
I can go without eating for a while, but my sister cannot. I
do it myself because I want to fulfill her goals, not all of
her dreams, but the home of them, and I want her to
study so that she does not have to witness all of this in her
future, which I am seeing and confronting right now.

Tears welled up in her eyes as she thought back on all her issues and compared them to her orphan friend's single issue. The poor girl temporarily altered her life, but as time went on her issues and obligations grew steadily more serious. She finished her education with great marks and grades. And finally, here is the time when she must handle all of her obligations.

"The day when you have to abandon all your tantrums is the day when you graduate from childhood to maturity."

Responsibility of an adult

She is now an adult, unemployed, and is viewed by others as nothing more than a useless person. Her parents are constantly concerned for her, and she feels hopeless on the inside as well. Relatives pressurize her, saying things like, If you are an unemployed person you should get married. Every day she receives jeers from everyone, and she also has weird delusions

that she has murdered someone. She desires to go for a solo walk outside to enjoy her own company. However, she is unable to go or fulfill her desires.

Why?
Due to the fact of society, evil monsters are waiting outside that are constantly ready to tease her, devour her flesh, and tear her to pieces. She feels a sense of pride in

the fact that her heart still functions despite having been burned, played with, stabbed, and damaged.
She is simply waiting for the day when she can leave the house without worrying, without having to deal with comments and glares from others, and the day when she feels appreciated and cared for.
She then started to cry in her tears of frustration.
She had transformed into a flower, Aconite(monkshood), a flower without scent and color.

"Not all flowers have good meanings and the Aconite is one of the exceptions. This pretty-looking flower is meant for hatred".

She is terrified of being judged by others and of everything else. She desires some quiet time to reflect in the dark and at last she understood what depression meant. Her parents hoped that their daughter should fulfill all their dreams because she owes them for all the years they raised her.

Knock knock! Someone opened the door
"Hey, my darling, why are you sobbing? Have confidence, daughter, everything will be okay", her mother remarked as she gave her a firm hug.

"A mother's kiss or hug is the purest thing to experience; it doesn't matter how old you are or how crucial it is."

For a while, she temporarily forgot about everything Mom said: "Nettom (her name), stop sobbing. I'm leaving for a few days; take care of everything here", and she leaves. Nettom visits numerous locations in search of employment but is consistently turned down she doesn't know why, as she is pretty intelligent but still she is rejected. She felt disappointed in herself as well. She feels she is a wretched girl who is constantly rejected and mistreated by everyone as she sits on the stairs of a store. Then a boy arrives and sits down next to her, asking her what the trouble is and why she is perplexed. The girl hurriedly gets up and leaves but the guy follows her.

Boy: Nettom stop! Girl: Hey
Girl: How did you get my name and who are you? Boy: Maybe your well-wisher!
Girl: I don't need somebody to wish me well. Please explain how you know my name.
Boy: Let me know what the issue is, and I'll respond to your query Girl: Thank you, girl! Just go out of here; don't dare to follow me again. I don't want to listen right now.
Boy: No, he said, I'll follow you until you respond to my

inquiry, as though you were in peril.
Girl: Why are you meddling in my business when it is
mine?
Boy: I might be able to fix your issue, just as I did when I
was young. Girl: Calls him "Fiar," his nickname!
Boy: Exactly.
Nettom seemed shocked!

Sir: Hello, buddy. You look completely different. What are
you doing here? Is everything okay?
Boy: Yes Nettom everything is good.

She responds to the boy's subsequent query by sharing the events in her life.
says, "We'll catch up another day. I've to go. My mom isn't home, then she departs.

Boy: Goodbye (smiling).

Each time they run into one another, they become drawn to one another. The guy is in love with her, but he is afraid to tell her because he fears she will reject him.
Her phone starts to ring the next morning. Hello, who? We are from the company, ma'am, where you previously applied for a job.
Nettom: Yeah, am I selected? Yes, Ma'am, you've been hired

The girl is now excited and pleased to have finally gotten a job. She initially gives his friend a call and enthusiastically announces, "I've finally obtained a job, and I'm glad right now."
Boy: Wow, that's excellent.
The Fair is now considering that because of her improved mood, I should inform her and show my love to her whether she accepts or not. The door is knocked on.
Girl: Hey Fiar,
Boy: Is everything okay?
Girl: Yes, everything. I'm here to inform you that my family decided to throw a small celebration for everyone

because I obtained a job.

She also wants you to come and enjoy it with us. Please join us for the celebration.
Boy: Yeah, why not. It is your first achievement and if you're inviting me to such a celebration, how can I say no? (both of them chuckle). Can I tell you something?
Girl: Sure, you can! Boy: Really?
Gir: Come on, man, feel free to share.

Then Fiar grabbed her hand and said, actually I want to say that we were good friends from childhood and I want to change this friendship into a strong relationship.
Girl: What do you mean by that, I do not understand!
Boy: "I love you and I really like you!" (He completely articulates his feelings.)
The girl left without responding after being frightened. She goes to her home and tells her mother that Fiar will not come. He is busy with his office work. At the night came all the guests, relatives, neighbors, and friends came but Nettom was still waiting for Fiar but he didn't come.

The next morning
Nettom entered the office, but she missed the boy. On the other hand, the boy was really upset.
The boy calls Nettom, but she doesn't answer.
Fiar was able to meet the girl while sobbing uncontrollably and said "I love you, Nettom, and all I desire is to be with you. (With tears in her eyes.)" The girl said, "I was waiting for you last night but you didn't come, may I know why?"
Boy: Did you miss me? Girl: No!
Boy: Okay, but why you left me there when I expressed my feelings?
Girl: Because I was not able to answer your question so I...

Boy: Can you give me it now?

Nettom: Ok! I also admit that I like you

Fiar: But when I admitted why didn't you answer that time? Nettom replied: I wanted to play with you, and secondly, I couldn't tell you that I also like you (blushing) so I left.

Both of them are currently enjoying a great relationship free of conflict or anything else. The qualityoflife was wonderful just now. Genuine love is always extremely valuable and selfless. They were not hiding anything from each other. But Nettom was possessive of him, she doesn't want to share him with anyone and can't see him with any other person.

But after two years, both were extremely busy with their lives and only had one or two hours to spend together, which they also had to share with their families. However, she is genuinely in love with him and would do anything to stay with him. Despite her best efforts to diffuse the issue, she fails. They continue to argue every day. Day by day, things were getting worse. Because of this, the girl was experiencing mental trauma and she began sobbing in dimly lit spaces. She had severe depression; the situation also frightened her family. Her family was worried about the weird things she was doing. Nettom used to like being alone, but now she worries that being by herself makes her feel uncomfortable. She tells Fiar everything. Although her situation was critical and it appeared that she was dealing with serious issues, he advised her not to take stress or anything else. When she speaks to anyone now, she becomes frustrated and hostile.

You are all aware of the annoying and uninteresting messages that occasionally appear on social media, and 70% of people would rather ignore them than interact with them. However, there are situations when you utilize these types of applications to feel better and to keep your mind fresh when using social media.

She started utilizing her phone, social media, music, and other things to make herself feel better. One day while contemplating her condition and way of life in her cabin, she felt depressed and took out her phone. She checked that a boy has been messaging him for the last 2 years. She now responds to him and asks him what his issue is. She doesn't want to talk to him and bids him farewell when he says, "I simply want to chat to you." but she ignores the chat.

Fiar and Nettom are arguing once more. Nettom thinks that he doesn't care

He is aware of my health, but he still behaves like he doesn't care about that. Cruel words and responses will eventually kill me. She tells him, "I don't want to talk to you," stating that they both have a bad attitude and know how much they will miss one another.

When attitude enters your head, it utterly ruins everything.

When Nettom sees his(boy's) message once more, she becomes even more enraged than before.

Gir: Why are you bothering me Nettom? Boy: Why aren't you talking to me, boy?
Girl: I think that my life is my own, and I have the freedom to do anything I choose.
Boy: I'm aware that it's your life, but what's wrong with me?

Because I understand why you do all of these cheap things, the girl said. I don't want a boy since they're all the same.

Boy: Can't we speak in a kind manner? Nettom: No.

Boy: Why?

Girl: Are you the one who was following me last time when I was shopping?

Boy: Yes!

Boy: Leave it, can we talk as a friend, please! The girl says bye without responding.

She now believes that she has a life, plenty of money, a house, and a job, but nothing makes her happy. With each passing day, Nettom found it harder to ignore Fiar. She ignores everything to feel better and responds to the boy's message. Both of them begin conversing with one another. The girl informs her that because they are only friends and she is already in a relationship, she asks her not to try to turn their friendship into something greater. On the other side, Fiar learns that Nettom speaks to that person without informing me, that she is having an extramarital affair with me. He travels to meet her and asks everything to her why she is acting in this way. The Fiar comes out, beckons, and says he's waiting for you outside. Nettom appears. Fiar (glumly): Who is he?

Nettom: who?

Boy: You know very well whom I am talking about. Nettom is acting strangely because she wants to make him envious, therefore she didn't respond.

Fiar: (shocked) He smacks her after becoming enraged. Why did you cheat on me and why did you speak to him without letting me know?

Nettom becomes upset and enraged, and she responds by telling him his identity as who you are. (in anger) and said you have no control over yourself cause he smacked her for the first time. She

departs after telling himshe won't forgive or forget. Fiar thinks that they are in a relationship, and in order to hide it and contour the ego she left.
Talking to that social media boy makes her feel a bit better. She gradually describes herself as a friend.

The boyadvises her to call him(Fiar) immediately because he could be wounded as well and wants to talk to her.
He has a phone, therefore he can call me too. Why me constantly? Boy: Put your ego aside and call him. Maybe everything will work out well.
The boy encourages her to contact him even though he knows he loves her and wants to make her happy at all times.
Girl: (Misses him) What should I do?
But she had no idea what would happen in the future because she was not aware of anything. She departs for home.
She is seated on the roadside and thinks about it. Her friend arrives.
Nettom: What are you doing here?

Boy: I was just going away when I spotted you. I must have stared at you for at least 20 minutes, as though you were contemplating something.
Nettom: Nothing.
Boy: Well, I believe you're not yet at ease with sharing.
Nettom: Actually, I was considering what to do next. I believe he has lost interest because he no longer thinks(cares) about me. Boy: "No, you weren't thinking about that," to which the indignant girl responds, "I told you; are you telling me that I'm lying?"
No, I'm sorry, boy. Nettom: huh!
Boy: You ought to try calling him once. I believe he misses you as well.
Girl: (rudely) I don't need your opinion; it scarcely has any value.

Boy: Feels hurt but again asks her to try once, only for me.
Girl: You know what I was pondering killing myself!
Woah, what about your family, the boy said.
Woman: Mmm! That is why I am unable to accomplish this. Silently, the guy walks away.
Hoping that Fiar will call her, the girl. She waited for him to call or initiate contact for five days, but he never did. She falls into a deep depression. After crying and screaming all night, she eventually decided to change her attitude and called him. When he didn't answer, she became even more upset. Her family is increasingly worried about her mental health. Her mother advised her to take a few days rest and she might want to visit a doctor.
She writes a message and sends it to the Fiar in which she

expressed her affection for him and how important he is to her and her life in the letter. She also says, I attempted to call you, but you didn't return my call. and now I'll try to call you just if I only have a few

Fiar: She's also hurt, therefore I should contact her. When he calls her, their conversation resumes, but this time there is notthesame joy and enthusiasm.Bothofthem experienceanger at times because she spoke to the guy, who is now her friend, and he teases her once again. The girl gets hurt. Repeatedly, fiar makes fun of her. She informs him, "I don't feel good, and I become angry about little things. I don't know what's wrong with me, and I have no control over myself. I beg you not to say those things because they will just make me feel worse. The doctor also said that because of your stress, you may have heart problems, and you should forget about anything that makes you feel down to make treatment easier. He also said that, in my opinion, if you consistently experience stress, your mind will suffer and you run the risk of becoming irrational. Fiar becomes worried about what is going on with her and begins to cry. He then asks him, "What are you thinking that makes you ill?

As she has informed him, she has no control over her, so she responds, "I don't know. I am experiencing insecurity, but I am not sure what is causing it. I'm troubled and restless. My head is clouded and my heart is heavy, but I'm at a loss for words. Despite wanting to speak up, I find it difficult to do so. At the same time as I need someone to hold me, everyone around me is starting to annoy me. I don't want to hear any voices or send any texts in response. I have no idea what I desire. I'm only caught up with myself". She is told by the guy not to worry because he will always be by her side.

"Fair, listen, I don't want to go because I genuinely love you. You are the one person I truly admire outside of my family. So, it's better to forget everything that has happened in the past". Fair concurs with her and encourages her to forget everything. As they were talking merrily. He promises her that he will never leave her. I'll always be there for you when you need something or anything else.

One day while they were just talking, Fiar asked her, "Why did you talk to him and why don't you tell me about it?" Nettom simply stated that I was speaking to him normally, but as the conversation deteriorated, they once more began to argue. Stop Fiar, Nettom commanded, but Fiar persisted, having the girl afraid of experiencing the same thing. The male teases her once again out of rage as the situation worsens, nevertheless, he has no idea that doing so may wreck her life. The girl is severely affected and refuses to speak to him, just crying and telling him, "I told you I'm not feeling well. Don't say something that will make me feel worse". She concludes by saying, "You will regret it, but the time will be gone, I promise!" and switches her phone off.

But she becomes unwell and starts puking. Her oxygen levels also drop as a result of her stress.

he now thinks that she is living a sad existence. She is useless, and so is everything she does. Her life is filled with sadness because where her name ends(M) there is the beginning of MELANCHOLY.

She still loves him even though she is aware of his lack of concern. She waits for him to come to her day and night, but nothing ever works out in her favor, but she still loves him unconditionally. She decides that she will call him and tell him we should fix it all and live a peaceful and happy life again. When she calls him he doesn't pick up, she calls him again and again but he still doesn't pick up her call. She sends him a message that we should fix it and all that but he ignores she tells him why are you ignoring; fine it's mine mistake I am sorry but he replies that I want over it here I don't you anymore in my life, I am breaking this relationship here and don't dare to text or call me again, we will be in contact but not in a relationship and you'll not interfere in my life also and says bye without listening to her.

She can no longer do anything that she previously could have done but in return, she has been torn to bits, and as a result, she is completely damaged. She only wants to see him happy, therefore she cut ties with him because she was aware that he no longer desired her presence in his life. She sobs her heart out in the hopes that he will one day return to her. In the hopes that one day he will return to her life and make the same efforts to keep her in it as she makes to maintain him, she respects his terms and conditions over her self-respect.

She starts writing everything to let her partner and society know what her life is like because "The word hell is formed from observing her life," she says. Although she is greatly loved by her *friend, when they converse, she insults him, makes him feel hurt, furious, mad, and sad, and warns him not to communicate with me. If anyone reads this, please tell my family that I am massacring myself because I can't take the stress any longer; if I don't, I'll become frustrated. And tell my neighbors that I am leaving this world as you've always told me you wished that I was never born. She tosses her book out the window and commits suicide*

A girl came across it, read it, and published it to let the world know what is happening to girls and women. Before publishing, she adds some paragraphs more.

<u>*And writes*</u>

Suicide cannot be a solution to any problem. The majority of suicides are caused by transient depression or despair. We found that most of us are killing ourselves because we can't face problems.

We want to give up when a sense of helplessness and isolation overtakes us. However, there can never be a justification for suicide that is morally acceptable. There is a method to continue facing life, even though it isn't easy. However, one must be at least willing to attempt. This bullshit is fake. Love someone even when you don't want to and even when dealing with them is difficult. Sometimes loving them is difficult. That's all there is to realist crap. If someone makes you feel undesired, don't go because you want to make them feel bad or guilty—they won't—leave because you no longer have a reason to be there. You must occasionally stand up for yourself. In the end, what is supposed to be goodwill succeed, and what is not, won't. Love is worth fighting for, but there are moments when you can't fight alone. Sometimes you need somebody to stand up for you. If not, you simply have to accept that what you provided them was more than they were prepared to give you and go on. I'm gradually realizing that no matter how we react, nothing will realize that life is best lived when you focus on your internal change; no one will suddenly feel bad for you because you ignored his/her flaws—rage, selfishness, and his inability to love anyone but himself. She had the option of having anyone in the world, but she always chose him. All that she was at this point was a scar on her chest, a crease in her past, and a memory that vanishes even faster than a hidden snapshot. Perhaps her partner is regretting it now, but time has passed. Every relationship will eventually become monotonous after a while. Love is a commitment to show your love physically and emotionally every day; it is not a feeling. It's challenging; there aren't always smiles, grins, and good times. People frequently give up when the fun stops and look for someone else because "the spark is gone," but that is not how it works. If someone truly cares for you and loves you without conditions, they will also adore and respect you, and no one will suddenly change their opinion of you. Sometimes it's better to just leave things as they are, let people go, struggle for resolution, don't look for solutions, and don't expect people to comprehend your perspective. I'm rapidly experiencing rather than what is going on outside of you. Improve your inner calm and self-awareness. You'll lose patience with a lot of people out of rage, hurt, disappointment, or just mood swings. But in life, it's about sticking with the ones who will fight beside you. People that remain with you despite having every motive to depart are to be valued. "Please put your own needs first. As fleeting as individuals are, don't allow them to become your entire universe. Own your actions and preferences. Don't take care of their needs. Work on yourself. I can assure you that they will depart, so don't stay around for them or give your all for them. Please, Living for oneself. Believe in yourself, you can do anything whatever you want to do, it's just a matter of confidence and self-respect. When someone acts as though they have numerous options, take yourself out of the equation and help them make a decision. No matter how much you care, there are times when you have to strive to not care. Because sometimes the people who mean the most to you can make you feel almost nothing. It's self-respect, not pride. Do not surround yourself with negative people if you want to experience great improvements in your life. Give no one in your life a full-time position who works part-time. Never accept anything less than what you deserve; know your worth and what you can contribute. You don't know your worth if you believe you can't survive without him/her. When you ask your parents how important you are, they should respond appropriately and accurately. I want you to think about your parents, they raised you and what they want from you is to see you happy and successful in your life, your future is their legacy. Make them feel proud of you, not ashamed. Before committing suicide think about you and your parents, you will not be able to weep their tears when they are crying at your funeral think about what will happen to them after your death, you don't want to end your life you only want to end your pain.